Also by D. W. Grant

POETRY

Shades of Life

Echoes of Life

Silence of Life

M. A. G. A.

*Making
America
Go Awry*

*Essays and Poems on
the State of the Union*

D. W. Grant

This is a work of fiction, except for the non-fiction parts. The opinions expressed are of the author alone. The names and places are fictitious except when referencing real events and places. For a definition of satire see any dictionary.

awry

adverb or adjective_
\ ə-ˈrī
\

Definition of *awry*

1 **:** off the correct or expected course **:** amiss
Their plans went awry.

2 **:** in a turned or twisted position or direction **:** askew
His wig was put on all awry, with the tail straggling
about his neck.— Charles Dickens
— From Merriam-Webster Online Dictionary.

Table of Contents

Introduction

Our Founding Fathers had a vision. They wanted to establish a country where the most important aspects were life, liberty, and the pursuit of happiness. They wanted a government of and for the people. However, they were smart enough to realize people as a group have a hard time governing themselves let alone keeping things equal. So, they set our nation up as a Republic, where people would elect representatives to do the actual governing and make the decisions that ensured the ideals the Founding Fathers had established would be carried out.

This was a great, if not revolutionary, idea and assumed that those elected would be of such character as to see that all persons were treated equally and the nation would live happily ever after. What they did not foresee, was what would happen if those in power were totally corrupt, inept, and without a moral compass. Which brings us to today.

In Bernard-Henri Lévy's book, *The Empire and The Five Kings*, he tells the story of Xenophen writing about Pericles the Younger who said, "the character of those who defend the laws is more important than the laws themselves." This rings loudly as today we watch politicians who have no character trampling over the laws of the land. Also what may be even worse, we have judges without character interpreting and setting the laws for all of us.

This compilation is a sometimes serious look into our current political situation, and a sometimes tongue-in-cheek satirical jab at our politicians. Sadly some of it is focused on our inability to have the guts to enact reasonable gun control. The essays and poems are reactions to the events and issues that have occurred over the last couple of years. My intention is to make you laugh, weep, and hopefully, think.

The Transition

One man leaves another comes in.
The question is, at what cost?
Values, morals, traditions once
honored, are now lost.

The lid to Pandora's box
has been raised.
Misogyny, bigotry, ignorance,
are now things to be praised.

Facts have become lies,
Lies are now truth.
Science is now bunk.
Lies believed without proof.

To speak out, to question
brings down wrath.
Anyone who disagrees asked
to leave, to take a different path.

Debate, discussion have become
things of the past.

One hundred forty characters are
all that will last.

One man leaves who was honorable,
very few were greater.
One man comes in, a narcissist,
con artist, and a traitor.

Whether we agree, or not,
regardless of our position.
It might behoove us all
to brush up on our Russian.

On The Eve of Destruction

Twas the night before the inauguration, and in almost
every house
People were asking themselves, "Who elected this
louse?"
Those who had been insured through Obamacare
Were worried it would no longer be there.

The children were terrified, their parents afraid,
Bills were piling up, there were debts to be paid.
They knew the rich would be the only ones to see,
The tax breaks that had been promised to you and to
me.

Everyone began to realize the lies that had been told,
A bill of goods we all had been sold.
There was never an intention of draining the swamp,
The "make us great" had all been pomp.

The reigns were being passed from one with class
To a narcissist who is totally crass.
A misogynist, a con-man, a bore,
One who may cause a nuclear war.

The fuhrer had gathered his cabinet,
Although they hadn't been approved just yet.
There was Tillerson, Zinke and Sessions.

Chao, Puzder and Carson,
Mnuchin, Shulkin, and McMahon,
Pruitt, Mulvaney, and Haley,
And let us not forget who brings up the rear,
Trade representative, Robert Lighthizer.

So as darkness fell awaiting the dawn.
We all laid awake, not even a yawn.
The next four years were full of doubt,
A buffoon is our president, only one way out.

So prayers are lifted hoping to God to reach,
Our only hope is for Congress to impeach.
So to all on the left or the right,
Sleep well, have a good night!

Ode to 45

Roses are red
Violets are blue
I didn't vote for Trump
Did you?

Donald and Mike took over the hill
Although liars, I guess it didn't matter.
We would love to bring them down,
But as of yet, their just getting fatter.

McConnell and Ryan have stopped the clock
The government is closed, shutdown
Both sides not willing to back down
The whole thing is a crock.

Women are marching two by two
Some for equality, some for #MeToo,
Whatever the reason, one thing for sure,
Republicans, brace yourself, come November, you're
through.

Donald is wishing he never met the porn star
Wish he may, wish he might
Although paid off, she is not going into the night.
Just maybe, this time, he went too far

Congress should be quick,
No time to quibble
Let's impeach this fraud,
We have enough to make it stick.

I know if you asked people, if you took a poll
There are enough sane ones left
Who listen to facts, who are not deaf,
Wanting to save us from becoming a shithole.

In spite of it all, we have high hopes
Like the little train that could
We not only think, we know
Yes, we can get rid of this dope.

Frumpty Trumpty

Frumpty Trumpty tried to build a wall

Frumpty Trumpty wanted it thirty feet tall

All the Republicans and all the Maga hats

Couldn't come up with the money,

and that was that.

The New National Anthem

Per executive order 432.1, dated February 2, 2017, I,
Donald J.Trump proclaim the following as the new
national anthem of the United States of America.
Heretofore to be sung at all public gatherings, sporting
events, and school assemblies.

Oh, hey, can you agree,

that The Donald's so bright.

And so proudly we hail

at all of Trump's streaming.

Whose broad ban and bold strokes,

we promise not to fight

And under Bannon's constant watch,

we're so gratefully beaming.

With the borders secure,

the Muslims no longer here.

Giving proof thro' the night

that our flag is still pure.

O hey, does that nationalistic banner show our might

O'er the land for those like us and the home of the right.

The New Pledge of Allegiance

The esteemed president of the United States, Donald Trump, has designated January 20 as Patriot's Day, to hereafter be celebrated by all loyal Americans. By executive order president Trump has declared the removal of the old pledge of allegiance from all buildings, schools, and historical records. The old pledge is to be replaced by the following new alternative pledge, and is to be recited daily by all citizens of these United States.

I pledge allegiance to Donald Trump,

Ruler of what was once the United States of America,

And to the "Make America Great Again" slogan for which he stands.

Although we are a divided nation, no longer under God, split asunder by hatred and bigotry,

We have liberty for all, except Muslims, the LGBT community, immigrants, and anyone he disagrees with,

And we have justice for all, except blacks, Hispanics, women, and reporters.

If Only We Believed the Pledge of Allegiance

Ironically, it was in January 2017 when I blogged about the new pledge of allegiance under Individual #1. What I did not realize, was just how prophetic it was, and how many purported United States citizens would live as if they believed it over the real one.

Now, in 2019, I think it is time to remind ourselves what the original says and what it means for this country. Thirty-one words that define what it means to be an American, words that if we really did believe them, would go a long way to healing this nation.

Stop any ten people on the street and I doubt any one of them would know the history of the pledge and I am not sure just how many would be able to recite the words. The pledge was the brain child of Francis Bellamy, a minister, who in 1892 wrote it hoping citizens of any country could use it. The original simply said:

"I pledge allegiance to my Flag and the Republic for which it stands, one nation, indivisible, with liberty and justice for all."

In 1923 it was changed to read:

"I pledge allegiance to the Flag of the United States of America and to the Republic for which it stands, one nation, indivisible, with liberty and justice for all."

And finally in 1954 the words *under God* were inserted giving us the version many of us recited every day in school. One thing I did not know, is that the controversy over making students recite the pledge started as early as 1935,[1] long before these two words were added. There have been many challenges over the years[2], but today one does not have to stand nor recite the pledge if they so choose. That however, is not the point of this blog.

Let us examine what the words say and is the pledge worth preserving!

It is fitting that the first word is "*I*". Each of has a responsibility as to what kind of country we are. It is easy to sit back and let other people take the reins, but as individuals, we each are responsible. The most significant way this manifests itself is in voting. The adage, every vote counts, could not be more true than in today's political environment. It is tempting to want

---

[1] See the New York Times article by Douglas Martin, September 6, 2014, "Lillian Gobitas Klose, 90, Dies; Stood Against Mandatory Pledge".

[2] See blog post by Scott Bombay, June 14, 2018, "The History of Legal Challenges to the Pledge of Allegiance."

voting to be mandatory, like in Australia, but more important, is an informed electorate. In 2016, 58% of eligible voters went to the polls, while high for an election, it says a lot about the apathy of the other 42%.

The word *pledge* is from the Latin, *plebium*, to undertake, to make a serious promise to do what comes after. Obviously, 42% per cent of citizens did not take it seriously in 2016.

Allegiance: loyalty or commitment to a superior or to a group or cause. This one is the biggie. It is what caused the first challenge to be brought before the Supreme Court (see the note above). If we are to be honest, what this means is more of a commitment to one's country, again voting being a good example of showing commitment.

To the flag: this is where the rubber meets the road. While our flag is special and there are rules about its use and care, it is a symbol. The problem is the meaning of that symbol has changed and been compromised[3]. The note is to a blog I wrote on July 4th, 2012. Sadly the division I described regarding our flag has widened. Once a symbol of a country united it is now used to rip us apart.

---

[3] See my blog post on July 4, 2012, "Why I Don't Fly the American Flag", on Dr Don's Diatribe.

of the United States of America: As the flag has become a symbol of division, this country is no longer united, but split into red and blue, and like the wall 45 would love to build, it seems we are unable to get over our differences.

and to the Republic: This may be one of the more important parts of the pledge. It reminds us that we are not a democracy, but a republic. To know the difference[4] is to understand what is wrong with our current political mess. The key being a constitution that guarantees the same rights to all citizens, which currently is not the case, at least in practice.

for which it stands: Where once this meant that America was a place that the world could look to for leadership, inspiration, support, and hope: the last two years have eroded that image. Maybe it is time for all of us to take a knee!

one nation,: As has been said in many ways above, we are far from being one nation and have definitely been divided. One nation does not mean we all have to agree, but when those disagreements tear into the fabric of who we are, then we have a problem. When we

---

[4] For good discussion on this see the article on Diffen.com entitled "Democracy vs. Republic."

refuse to listen to opposite opinions or fail to try to see the other side of an issue, we are beyond repair.

under God: I am surprised that this was allowed to be put in. The Constitution is clear regarding the separation of church and state. The problem as I see it is that while God is not defined, the implication of it being a Christian God has taken hold and perpetuates the false idea that this is a Christian nation.

indivisible: This word means unable to be divided or separated. In the current political climate, this small word is almost laughable. We are more divided than ever, at least more than I can ever remember. Yes, we had division in the Civil War, and have always had differing view points, but the gap today seems almost wider than ever. For the United States to be what it was meant to be, this is the biggest hurdle to overcome.

with liberty and justice for all: The irony of this is many who would insist the pledge be recited, who stand up when we play the national anthem, are the last to live by these final words. White supremacy, anti-immigration, anti-Muslim, love it or leave it, are ideas and beliefs that undermine the concepts of liberty and justice for all. The us and them mentality takes the wind out of the sails of the ship of liberty and justice. As Leonard Cohen says in his poem, *Democracy* -

"Sail on, sail on, O mighty Ship of State!
To the Shores of Need Past the Reefs of Greed
Through the Squalls of Hate
Sail on, sail on, sail on, sail on".

Imagine a country where the words to our pledge were taken to heart, implemented and practiced in everyday life. A country that raised the flag as a symbol of hope, equality, justice, respect, and liberty. A nation, undivided, indivisible. A country that symbolizes what a people can become when all are treated fairly. Imagine the United States of America as it was meant to be. That will be the day the pledge of allegiance becomes worthy of recitation.

Trump's Letter to His Succesor

George Bush Sr. wrote a great letter to Clinton at the end of his term. We just discovered a draft of #45's letter to his successor.

Dear Next President (who won because 5 million immigrants voted illegally),

When I walked into my office, I realized I am the best President ever, no doubt, believe me. You will never be as great as me.

You will wish you were as great as me, but sadly, there is only one Donald and that would be me. I never felt alone here, because I was always with me, and who could ask for a better companion. Plus I had a direct line to my best buds Vladimir and Sean.

There will be many fake news stories about me and people who were not loyal (most of whom are now in jail).

My advice would be to listen to your gut. I know my gut knows more than my brain and I can hear my gut talk to me (especially after I eat Big Macs and fried chicken).

When you read this you will think I am gone, but not really, I will never leave, don't tell anyone (especially Melania) but I am hiding in the Blue Room which I am painting gold.

You will never be as successful as me, so sad.

Good luck with that umbrella.

DJT (the best president ever)

We Have Forgotten

Every September 11, if you have been on Facebook, Twitter, other social media, or god forbid, read a newspaper, you have probably seen the remembrance of 9/11/01 with the slogan, "We will never forget". The only problem with that is we have.

When the two planes struck the towers at the World Trade Center, and we heard the news of the third plane going down in Pennsylvania, and the plane hitting the Pentagon, the country for a short time was united. We grieved for the loss of life, we were outraged that America had been attacked, we turned to each other for comfort, strangers shared emotions and racial lines blurred. We wanted to know who was responsible and we wanted to avenge the deaths of so many.

Our emotions blinded us into believing the government when we were asked to go to war. So once again we sent sons and daughters into battle. The world stood by us and joined in the fight for retribution. Little did we know, that like Vietnam, we were being duped. The weapons of mass destruction were non-existent and we found ourselves in a quagmire that continues even today.

The event that brought us together has been forgotten. Our nation is divided more than it ever was. The world no longer looks to us for leadership. Our government is failing on so many levels. And we have a narcissistic moron in the White House.

Hatred, bigotry, racism, and division are worse than ever. Actually, that is not true. They are simply more obvious and blatant. Fueled by the rhetoric of an ignorant con man, groups and individuals who lurked in the shadows or under rocks have come out in the open. They spew hatred and division as much as they can. People are openly disrespecting each other based on skin color, accent, or for just being different.

Even the definition of what is an American patriot has dissolved into whether or not one kneels for the national anthem. A nation built on debate, compromise, and unity has become a nation of bitterly divided opinion, lack of respect for each other, and unwillingness to compromise. We have forgotten.

September 11, 2001 brought out the best in the people of this nation. It is sad that only a short time after we are seeing the worst.

Why, Why Did America Die

My apologies and thanks to Don McLean for the use
and inspiration respectively of one of the greatest songs
of our time. *American Pie*, released in 1971.

It doesn't seem that long ago
Even though it's hard to remember now
That this country was doing okay.
Things weren't perfect by any means
Back when I was in my teens
But things have changed since that day.

But January 2017 made us worse
That's when we came under a curse
Fake news became a reality
Truth and facts a casualty.

I can't believe things are this bad
To see democracy fall is so sad
One man who constantly lied
Has caused democracy to die.

Oh Why, why did America die?
Drove my Honda to the station
But gas was too high
And fascists were spewing prejudice and lies
Yelling make America white again
This was the day democracy died.

Hypocrites quote the Bible with ease
To justify positions as they please
Taking verses out of context
Ignoring all the rest
They believe God is on their side
But forget why Christ died.

Well, I know it won't be that long
That Trump-ets will sing a different song
Cause what they fail to remember
Is we will all vote come November.

Teenagers are mobilizing in mass
Signing voters, kicking ass
Politicians no longer get a pass
Maybe democracy doesn't have to die
But we're still singin'

Why, why did America die?
Drove my Honda to the station
But gas was too high
And fascists were spewing prejudice and lies
Yelling make America white again
This was the day democracy died.

Now, for two years they have been in control
The hate and division are taking their toll
But, that is not how it needs to be.

The clown is sitting in the Oval Office
Orange and fat, hating all of us
But now it's up to you and me

While he's spending time playing golf
Taking way, way too much time off
The voters will return
His kingdom about to burn

He likes to court Putin and Un
And wants us all to march to his tune
But forgets deep inside,
We will not let democracy die
We won't be singin'

Why, why did America die?
Drove my Honda to the station
But gas was too high
And fascists were spewing prejudice and lies
Yelling make America white again
This was the day democracy died.

He wants a parade in his honor
While affordable healthcare is a goner
But his policies will not last.

More players will refuse to stand
When the anthem is played by the band
Until prejudice is a thing of the past

The classroom was filled with shattered glass
The sound of gunfire, no one had a chance
Valentine's Day, cancel the dance
The only safe place, out on the grass.

The NRA stood steadfast.
Gun control will never pass
We will keep our guns at all cost
No matter how many lives were lost
And the students started singin'

Why, why did America die?
Drove my Honda to the station
But gas was too high
And fascists were spewing prejudice and lies
Yelling make America white again
This was the day democracy died.

So now we've come to this time and place
To ask what will the next generation face
Will democracy live again.

So hickory dickory dock
There is time left on the clock
The lies will come to an end

While he hides in Mar-a-Largo
It is time for him to go
The curtain will fall on his show
Just as winter brings the snow

And while he thought he was flying high
The voters will shoot him out of the sky
And he will crash and burn and that is why
we won't be singin'

Why, why did America die?
Drove my Honda to the station
But gas was too high
And fascists were spewing prejudice and lies
Yelling make America white again
This was the day democracy died.

The country will no longer sing the blues
and it will be the death of all the fake news
We all can laugh and play.

The people will go to the polls
And will find their names on the rolls
Democracy will be here to stay

And across the land the people cheered
No hate or prejudice appeared
Not an evil word was spoken
No one seen as just a token

And the values we hold so dear
Truth and justice once again were clear
Across the land you could hear
Democracy had not died

The people were singing'
My, my America didn't die
Drove my Honda to the station
And gas was not high
Fascists no longer spewing hatred and lies
This will be the day
Democracy does not die.

Sounds We Often Hear

Sounds we often hear
Aren't the sounds we actually hear.

Words can be said not very clear
Making us wonder, "What did I hear?"

Songs can be sung with words that are slurred.
We try to listen to hear what we've heard.

Some sounds are actually very clear,
Like the sound of brakes hitting us from the rear.

Some sounds confuse our ears,
We aren't really sure just what we hear.

Like a popping sound that was very near,
Was that a gun so close to my ear?

When the sounds stop and only silence we hear,
Fifty lay dead, it was a gun, now it is clear.

Why the Second Amendment Is Like the Bible

"A well regulated militia being necessary to the security of a free State, the right of the People to keep and bear arms shall not be infringed."

Amazing how so few words can create such controversy. Often misquoted, misused, and abused, this sentence has caused more confusion and delusion than the Bible. Well, okay, maybe not as much as the Bible, but still a lot. Like the Bible, words are taken out of context, used to defend a particular viewpoint, and open to interpretation. Like the Bible, the Second Amendment's meaning is layered.

When Bible scholars look at the meaning of a verse or passage, they ask three questions: What does the original say? What did it mean when written? And, What does is mean for us today? This approach could serve interpretations of the Second Amendment as well.

The question of what does the original say is easy as it stands today as written in 1791. It is interesting to note that the first draft said ..."*to the security of a free Country,*"...., and was changed to *free State* by the insistence of the southern states. The reason being, they

28

did not want government interference in the slave militias; patrols that kept slaves from rebelling and brought runaways back to their owners.

This helps us in interpreting the original intent. The right to bear arms was tied to a well regulated militia. Until 2008, the rulings of the Supreme Court centered around the idea of the militia. Ironically, for the discussions today, the case of United States vs. Miller[5] (1939) stated that a shotgun with a barrel less than eighteen inches was not protected under the Second Amendment saying, *"Certainly it is not within judicial notice that this weapon is any part of the ordinary military equipment, or that its use could contribute to the common defense."*

It was in 2008 when things changed. The Supreme Court ruled 5-4 in the case of District of Columbia vs. Heller that, *"We start therefore with a strong presumption that the Second Amendment right is exercised individually and belongs to all Americans."* What was still possible was the right to regulate fire arms in the case of "unusual" weapons, which is what the 1939 case had stated regarding sawed-off shotguns.

---

[5] See blog post by Tom Head, January 12, 2019 entitled "The Second Amendment and Gun Control."

Like the Bible, the Second Amendment has been co-opted by the far right. Extreme fundamentalists use a strict interpretation of the Bible, and anyone who disagrees is condemned. Sadly, this rule book approach has done more harm than good. As for the Second Amendment, the group that began as a safety and educational source for the proper use of firearms has become one of the most influential and feared political entities in the country. The NRA[6] went from its roots in 1871 of educating marksmen, to a political juggernaut that can make or break a candidate's chances of being elected.

Using fear to persuade people to believe that any regulation on firearms will lead to the removal of all guns and large amounts of money to line the pockets of lawmakers, the NRA has been successful in thwarting attempts to curb weapons such as assault rifles.

This stand is the same as creationists saying if you don't believe the world was created in six literal days then you are not a believer. While the Bible describes creation this way, science has proven that there is more to how the world came about than a few verses in

---

[6] See blog post by Ron Elving, October 10, 2017 entitled "The NRA Was Not Always Against Gun Restrictions."

Genesis state. Our knowledge has expanded opening up a different interpretation of the process.

In the same way, the availability of military-style weapons to the general public requires a re-examination of the meaning of the Second Amendment. The ideas of background checks, age limits, mental illness and national data bases, banning of assault weapons, banning bump stocks, do not infringe on the right to bear arms. My right to own a handgun or rifle is not thwarted by any of the above.

The real problem is one of dialog. Like gay rights, divorce, or interpretations of the Bible, it is hard to get religious people to agree or even listen to each other. More so with gun advocates and those wanting restrictions. Rather than intelligent conversations, both sides of any of these issues are too quick to resort to name calling or close-mindedness.

Maybe it is just human nature to think one side is right and one side is wrong. While this attitude in regards to the Bible results in heated debate and a plethora of denominations, sects, and cults, this division over the Second Amendment results in lives lost.

Them Used To Be Us

Webster defines immigrant as simply "a person who comes from another country to live in another one." This is as opposed to an emigrant who "is a person who leaves a country or region to live in another one." So the Pilgrims were emigrants when they boarded the Mayflower and immigrants when they landed at Plymouth Rock. Some will say unless you are a Native American you are either an immigrant or a descendant of one. Actually this is not true as even the Native Americans came from Northeast Asia[7] across the Bering Land Bridge approximately 25,000 years ago.

While all of this may be interesting, the current debate over immigration has America more divided than ever. Fueled by misinformation and fear, there are many who support a Muslim ban, a wall along our Mexican border and the end of DACA. There is a need for immigration reform but the current administration is pushing an agenda that is splitting families apart, inspiring hate crimes, asking the nation to spend 25

---

[7] Time Magazine article, July 21, 2015 by Tanya Basu entitled "There's a new theory about Americans' Native origins."

billion on a useless wall, and threatening to uproot those who were brought here as children and are now responsible adults within our society.

Those backing these policies have forgotten from whence they came. Sadly for them, there is Jennifer Mendelsohn. Through her site she calls #resistancegenealogy, she "has been using people's public family history to beat back some of the uglier claims about immigrants and how they fit into US history[8]." One of my favorites is about Vice President Mike Pence, who spoke out against so-called chain migration. The term "used by demographers since the 1960s to refer to the social process by which migrants from a particular town follow others from that town to a particular destination city or neighborhood." To hear those opposed to chain migration talk, they make it sound as if hordes of immigrants are swarming across our borders to live off taxpayers. The facts are somewhat different, I refer you to this New York Times article, "*What Is Chain Migration*, " January 26, 2018. But back to Pence. Through her research, Mendelsohn discovered, "VP Mike Pence is also the product of

---

[8] CNN article June 23. 2018 by A.J. Willingham entitled "They spoke out against immigrants. So she unearthed their own immigrant ancestors."

'chain migration'. His Irish grandfather arrived in 1923, with passage paid for by an older brother who'd arrived a few years earlier. Brother's passage had been paid for by an aunt. Let's stop pretending to be surprised."

It is perplexing to try and understand why most Republicans are anti-immigration. One answer, at least for those in Congress, comes from Robert Sapolsky's insightful book, B*ehave: The Biology of Humans at Our Best and Worst*. Based on what he calls social-dominance orientation (SDO), which is the measure of how much people value power and prestige, the higher one's SDO, the less likely one will feel empathy to the less fortunate. Neurologically, this is explained by those with a high SDO having low basal glucocorticoid levels which means less activation of the anterior cingulate cortex and insular cortex, both of which promote empathy. While this may help explain behavior, Sapolsky points out that this tells us nothing of which came first, the power position or the lack of empathy.

As for the rest of those in favor of a wall or a ban, Sapolsky would put them in the category of people who "often haven't a clue why they've made some judgement, yet they fervently believe it's correct." This is based on scientists who study moral behavior and conclude that we make moral decisions based on intuition. Then use reasoning to convince everyone, including ourselves, that we're making sense. My take would be that they get their "facts" from the likes of Fox News.

The group that perplexes me the most are Christians who back the anti-immigration rhetoric and/or still support the current occupant of the White House. As for my opinion on Christians and 45, I refer you to a previous blog, "It is a good thing Jesus resurrected.[9]" For those who rant about immigrants, there is one simple question. "What would Jesus do?"

Sadly, the bashing of immigrants is not new in the United States. Sometimes it is easy to forget history. There was an article from the Huffington Post on December 6, 2017 entitled "Ann Coulter's Immigrant Ancestors" that reminds all of us just how badly immigrants have been treated from the beginning of this great country we call America. Pence, being Irish, should read his own history[10].

The debate is getting hotter and politicized more than ever as this is being written. The stories of ICE

---

[9] Posted September 22, 2017 on Dr. Don's Diatribe.

[10] on History.com there is a story by Christopher Klein entitled "When America Despised the Irish: The 19th Century Refugee Crisis."

using, and abusing[11], the power this administration has given them, pile up every day. Republicans and Democrats are drawing lines in the sand to stake out their positions. One thing both sides, and all of us, need to remember: Immigrants, like the homeless, are not a category. They are human beings that need to be treated fairly and with compassion.

We used to be them!

[11] Washington Post article by Mick Miroff and Maria Sacchetti on February 12, 2018 entitled "ICE arrests of 'noncriminal' immigrants double under Trump."

Why God Made Trump President

Imagine you have been in a coma for five years. Some of the last things you remember are: the first *Hunger Games* movie was out, *The Dark Night Rises* with Christian Bale as Batman had been released, Apple had announced the iPhone 5, there had been a mass shooting in Newton, Connecticut at an elementary school called Sandy Hook, and Barack Obama had been elected to a second term.

It's possible the last thing you remembered was Tom Cruise being cast as Jack Reacher in the film based on the series by Lee Child. This last one may have been the reason you went into a coma, your mind could not comprehend Cruise as Reacher, a five foot-seven inch, one hundred-forty eight pound actor playing a character who is six feet-five inches, two hundred-fifty pounds.

Through the miracle of modern medicine, you have come out of your coma and it is 2017. You are going to have obvious questions about what has happened during your absence. You might ask is Christian Bale still playing Batman, only to find out that it is now Ben Affleck. As you start to fall back into a coma over that fact, you shake your head and ask about any new Apple products and are told the newest is the iPhone X.

Remembering the devastation of the Sandy Hook shooting you ask if there has been any progress on gun control. You learn that not only has there not been any changes but there have been one thousand-five hundred-fifty-eight mass shootings since. Or twenty-nine depending on one's definition[12] of what constitutes a mass shooting. With trepidation you ask who is the new president after Obama, and are told it is the real estate mogul and host of the *Apprentice*, Donald J. Trump. Realizing they are not joking, you then ask, "*Why*?"

Some would answer because he made campaign promises that resonated with a large part of America, people wanted change, they wanted to shake up the status quo. Others would say it was a backlash against Obama and people not wanting a woman as president. And then there are those that say God made Trump president.

---

[12] Time magazine article, October 2, 2017 entitled "Why Are There So Many Conflicting Numbers on Mass Shootings" by Chris Wilson.

Paula White, the leader of the New Destiny Christian Centre in Orlando Florida said[13], "Because God says that he raises up and places all people in places of authority, it is God who raises up a king. It is God that sets one down....Do I believe God raises up authority? Do I believe he sets one up and puts one down? I don't believe that just for Trump, I believe that had Hillary [Clinton] been in. I believe that for [Barack] Obama."

Franklin Graham, son of the evangelist Billy Graham, said[14], "I don't have any scientific information. I don't have a stack of emails to read to you. But I have an opinion: I believe it was God....He answered the prayers of hundreds of thousands of people across this land who had been praying for this country."

Former Minnesota congresswoman, Michelle Bachman went even further by saying[15] "God made

[13] Metro News blog September 11, 2017 by Ashitha Nagesh entitled "Donald Trump's 'spiritual advisor' believes God made him president."

[14] Blastingnews blog December 17, 2016 entitled "Christian extremist Franklin Graham awkwardly claims 'God' made Donald Trump president."

[15] The Daily Dot article on April 4. 2017 by Ana Valens entitled "Michele Bachman thinks God made Trump president to stop trans bathroom rights."

Trump president to prevent transgender people from using bathrooms that align with their gender identity."

The most dramatic statement came from Pat Robertson when he said[16] that anyone opposing Trump was revolting against God.

Even Trump, in a speech to the students at Liberty College said[17] that he had been elected with God's help.

While the extreme right wing of Christianity is rejoicing over the man they believe God appointed as savior for the United States, I am going to propose that maybe God did put Trump in the oval office, but for a different reason. My reasoning is more in tune with Obasanjo, the two time head of state of Nigeria. In a speech at the French embassy in South Africa he said, "The fact that America can produce a Trump in this day and age, it means Americans are as human as we are....Trump has come by Divine Will so that America can be humbled, and we can also learn a lesson." I would add, so we can learn several lessons. What better way to show the world who and what we should be than by giving us the extreme opposite.

---

[16] Snopes article by David Emery, February 16, 2017, entitled "Pat Robertson: Those Who Oppose Trump Are Revolting Against God's Plan."

[17] Time article, May 13, 2017, "Read Donald Trump's Liberty University Commencement Speech."

Proverbs 6:16-19 says --

"[16] These six things doth the Lord hate: yea, seven are an abomination unto him:[17] A proud look, a lying tongue, and hands that shed innocent blood,[18] A heart that deviseth wicked imaginations, feet that be swift in running to mischief,[19] A false witness that speaketh lies, and he that soweth discord among brethren."

Trump is narcissistic, a liar, divisive, misogynistic, a con man, and has no empathy for others. If God did put him in charge, is He trying to teach us something?

The first lesson being just who are we as humans and what is our responsibility to the planet we call home. Trump claimed that climate change was a hoax perpetuated by the Chinese. He has appointed climate change deniers to his cabinet, and is doing all he can to strip away environmental protections. He is adamant about bringing back coal and has backed out of the Paris agreement where the rest of the world had agreed to reduce emissions. This is the exact opposite of what God intended.

[26] And God said, Let us make man in our image, after our likeness: and let them have dominion over the fish of the sea, and over the fowl of the air, and over the cattle, and over all the earth, and over every creeping thing that creepeth upon the earth.

^{27} So God created man in his own image, in the image of God created he him; male and female created he them.

^{28} And God blessed them, and God said unto them, Be fruitful, and multiply, and replenish the earth, and subdue it: and have dominion over the fish of the sea, and over the fowl of the air, and over every living thing that moveth upon the earth. (Genesis 1:26-28, KJV).

Humans were given dominion over the earth. Unfortunately, the word dominion is often taken to mean destruction or doing whatever we want. The Hebrew word *radah* from which we get dominion, implies responsibility, treating as having value. God created heaven and earth and left us to maintain earth, to see that it is treated with respect and preserved. Not ravish and destroy it.

Imagine a lush green forest with clear water running through it—God's creation.. Now imagine the same scene stripped of vegetation and the river polluted from strip mining—Trump's creation. So by putting Trump in charge God is saying, "Wake up, I gave you dominion to respect and preserve my creation not destroy it." Because of Trump more of us are environmentally aware than ever before. More of us are taking action to preserve our natural resources, to protect the environment. The corruption of public officials who vote to ruin the environment after bribes from the oil and gas industry is being exposed more than ever.

The second lesson revolves around immigration. Trump campaigned on the promise to build a wall and to stop Muslims from coming to America. By claiming to make America great again, he basically was saying make America white again. Not only does this fly in the face of what this nation stands for, it goes completely against what God intended.

"For I was hungry and you gave me something to eat, I was thirsty and you gave me something to drink, I was a stranger and you invited me in." (Matt 25:35 NIV).

This verse is just one of many in the Bible talking about helping the poor, the refugee, anyone lest fortunate. Christians, especially, should be the first to advocate for the homeless, those forced to flee their home and country, the stranger that needs shelter.

Pope Francis said in October of 2016, "The world needs Christians to witness God's mercy through service to the poorest, the sick (and) those who have abandoned their homelands in search of a better future for themselves and their families. In putting ourselves at the service of the neediest, we will experience that we already are united; it is God's mercy that unites us."

Cities and states have become vocal in protecting immigrants, opening their arms to refugees. Even places like Missoula, Montana[18]_have committed to helping displaced foreigners. Thanks to Trump more Americans are honoring the plaque attached to the Statue of Liberty. Words from the poem *The New Colossus* by Emma Lazarus - "Give me your tired, your poor, Your huddled masses yearning to breathe free, The wretched refuse of your teeming shore. Send these, the homeless, tempest-tossed to me, I lift my lamp beside the golden door!"

The third lesson is one of morality. Trump represents the worst in moral values, treatment of women, respect for one's fellow man, and empathy to those who suffer.

From the golden rule, "Therefore all things whatsoever ye would that men should do to you: do ye even so to them."(Matt 7:12 KJV), to simply being kind

---

[18] The Missoulian article January 2, 2017 entitled "Missoula refugees now number 46."

to one another as written in Ephesians, God asks us to respect each other.

Thanks to Trump, and to Harvey Weinstein, sexual harassment is no longer being tolerated, and women are saying, "*Enough*!" As a country, we are having to ask ourselves what is acceptable and what is not. These are discussions long overdue, and may not have happened without the likes of Trump and his misogynistic outlook.

The final lesson is one of love. If there is any message in the Bible, it is that God is love. Christ left us with this one new commandment --

[34] "A new command I give you: Love one another. As I have loved you, so you must love one another. [35] By this everyone will know that you are my disciples, if you love one another." (John 13: 34-35 NIV).

What better way to show what love is than to lift up one so full of hate. Trump has exposed the underlying hatred that exists in this country and in trying to divide us, has caused more of us to unite and proclaim this is not who we are.

So thank God for making Trump president. Because of him, we are more aware of the condition of our planet, more concerned for those less fortunate, more aware of how we treat each other, and more vocal against those who hate. And hopefully, more politically aware as to never let the likes of Trump in the White House again.

If God did put Trump in the oval office, it was to make America great again, just not in the way Trump intended. Amen.

United We Stand, United Not So Much

"We hold these truths to be self-evident, that all men are created equal, that they are endowed by their Creator with certain unalienable Rights, that among these are Life, Liberty and the pursuit of Happiness."

The above quote is one we are all familiar with, it is part of the foundation upon which this nation was built. Setting aside the gender bias, it is meant to remind us all that no one of us is better or less than another. Part of the naming of this country included the word united, as in The United States of America. The question must then be asked, why are we doing so much to divide us?

America was built by people from all parts of the world. Germans, Irish, English, Chinese, Dutch, French, African (although not willingly), and Italian, just to name a few. Once here, and settled, all these nationalities became American. They did not give up their heritage but blended it with those around them and embraced this unique identity. Were there cultural clashes, bigotry, racism, divisions? Yes, but for the most part this country became a melting pot and an example of what a free society could be.

Today there are so many forces trying to divide us, to pit us against one another, it seems we are destined to fall apart. Whether it is political, religious, skin color, or economic, there is no end to reasons we can't use to separate ourselves from each other. One that puzzles me came up in a news story[19] about a woman registering her children for school.

The parent was asked not only to classify her child as Asian, but as to which Asian: Chinese, Japanese, Vietnamese, Filipino, Hawaiian, Samoan, or one of nine other choices. She responded by saying her children were born in the United States and are American. The school said that according to Assembly Bill 1088, government code 8310.5, the school is required to ask. The funny thing is that only Asians are subdivided. Under white, it does not ask German, Irish, English, Italian, etc.

While the reasoning for always having to classify ourselves on forms, government or otherwise, may be sound and of value, just doing so keeps us in a divisive mentality. Once an individual becomes a citizen, either

---

[19] The Mercury News article, June 27, 2017 by Angela Ruggiero, entitled "Asian parents demand race categories be removed…"

natural-born or otherwise, they are an American. When we lose sight of this fact, it is then division begins.

As Americans we can be Democrats, Republicans, Independents, Jews, Catholics, Protestants, Muslims, pro or anti abortion, pro or anti firearms, climate change deniers or believers, but no one is better than the other. The moment we use any category to claim superiority, we divide.

The current political climate seems hell bent on dividing us, inflamed rhetoric on both sides fuels the differences between us and tries to erase the fact that we are all Americans. It is too easy to fall into the trap of believing one group has the answers and another the cause of our problems. Rational discussion has become nearly impossible as both sides shout to be heard over the other. It reminds me of the Buffalo Springfield song, *For What It Is Worth,* where it says, "There's battle lines being drawn, nobody's right if everybody's wrong."

The Fourth of July is a day to celebrate our independence, maybe it is also a good time to reflect on who we are as a nation. We may have originally come from Europe, Asia, Africa, Australia, or some other part of the world, but as citizens we are all American. As

Aesop said in the fable of *The Four Oxen and The Lion*, "United we stand, divided we fall."

Why Trump Has Been Good for America

The Electoral College has placed Donald J. Trump in the presidential seat. In spite of the fact that the majority of Americans had a different idea, the reality is Mr. Trump sits as the 45th president of the United States. Whether this makes you mad or glad, either way the truth is, this is reality. Whether one looks at this as a good or bad thing is another matter.

It is easy to see the bad. We now have a babbling, narcissistic, misogynistic, lying, dictatorial, con-artist representing the greatest country in the world. Our allies are fearful, our enemies are emboldened, and our nation is divided more than any time in history, with possibly the exception of the Civil War. But before we all go running off to Canada, we need to realize how much good 45 has done for the good ol' USA.

Not since the Sixties have so many taken an interest in the politics of this nation. It has been easy for many of us to ignore much of what was happening in Washington, D.C., until now. Suddenly, people are talking, reading, and researching just how our government works. Copies of the Constitution are appearing in households where no book has darkened the door for years. Words like emoluments are rolling off tongues as easily as non-fat latte.

We are seeing the strengths and weaknesses of being a democracy. The system of checks and balances is keeping us from succumbing to a potential tyrant. At the same time, we are seeing the failure of career politicians who seemingly are more power hungry than concerned for the American people.

People who were content to sit idle, watching shows like American Idol, are now marching, rallying, calling, tweeting, and posting. They are speaking out, demanding that representatives, senators, and local politicians hear what they have to say.

In spite of the media being labeled "fake news", subscriptions to newspapers and viewership of nightly news programs are up[20]. People are reading more. The novel *1984* by George Orwell is so popular it is hard to find a copy in a brick and mortar bookstore or on Amazon.

The questions of who are we as Americans and what does this country stand for, are topics being examined as never before. The issues of racism,

---

[20] CNBC.com article, November 29, 2016 by Matthew J. Belvedere and Michael Newberg, entitled "New York Times subscription growth soars tenfold, adding 132,000, after Trump's win."

women's rights, religious freedom, and gender identity are at the forefront of daily discourse. The lid has been ripped off of previously hidden groups of fascists, racists, misogynists, and neo-Nazis.

Groups that fight daily for human rights, such as the ACLU[21] and Planned Parenthood[22], have seen donations increase in staggering amounts. Neighbors are organizing, forming grass root movements to figure out what they can do to make a difference. Some people are learning for the first time who their local and state government officials are, and are engaging in constructive dialogues.

The plight of immigrants, legal and illegal, is becoming more apparent. The reality of their contribution to this country is being made evident. Cities are stepping up and declaring themselves sanctuaries. Churches are opening their doors, that should have never been closed. Actually, a distinction is being made between those who only give lip service, and those who live as Christians.

---

[21] New York Times article, January 30, 2017 by Liam Stack entitled "Donations to A.C.L.U. and Other Organizations Surge After Trump's Order."

[22] The Blaze.com article, December 27, 2016 by Kate Scanlon entitled "Planned Parenthood claims massive spike in donations since Trump's election."

The final good thing has yet to be seen. The real good that could come out of 45 sitting in the Oval Office, would be for this nation to realize if we are to survive, if we are to remain a democracy, we need to be able to debate, discuss, disagree, yet somehow find a middle ground where everyone is respected, everyone is equal, and everyone working together can keep this country great.

Lest We Forget, Or Have We Already

Memorial Day is a time to pause and reflect, to honor and pay respect to those who fought and died, preserving this nation and the freedoms that we often take for granted. Men and woman who died to protect us from fascism, Nazism, communism, and the tyranny these ideologies promote. Sadly, it is tyranny that is once again at our door, this time from within.

Recently, I read and reviewed a small book entitled, *On Tyranny: Twenty Lessons From the Twentieth Century* by Timothy Snyder. I called this the second book all Americans should read, the U.S. Constitution being the first. The twenty lessons are to help us prevent tyranny from raising its ugly head here, allowing what all who have died to protect us, be for naught.

A patriot is defined as one who vigorously supports their country and is prepared to defend it against enemies or detractors. Maybe the key word here is vigorously. In the book, Snyder gives concrete examples of how we can be vigorous.

One point he makes that is worth reflecting on, especially today, is in lesson 18 - "Be calm when the unthinkable arrives." Snyder points out that "modern tyranny is terror management." When an event occurs, such as 9/11, it is easy for us to be willing to give up freedoms hoping to prevent a similar event. Think of all the things we used to be able to do, that have been taken away. From being able to walk a loved one to a boarding gate, to being able to enter a plane without being groped. These are minor compared to what could happen if we are not vigorous patriots.

History has shown that tyrants use such events to take control of governments and people. Hitler did this in Germany, Putin did this in Russia, Trump is attempting to do this here. To be fair, Trump is too stupid to do this, but his advisors are not, and his ego is allowing other tyrants, such as Putin, to pull him into terror management. In this case terror management being "the exploitation of real, dubious, and simulated terror attacks to bring down democracy."

Whether it is the Muslim ban or the border wall, alternative facts or discrediting the media, chanting "Lock her up" or denying climate change, we have a president seemingly determined to undermine the very freedoms the men and women who died, who we honor today, gave their lives to protect.

My hope is that as we reflect on the lives sacrificed for democracy, that we will become vigorous patriots. No longer content to sit on the sidelines, to simply hear opinions like our own, but to read for ourselves, to investigate truth, to seek out those who think differently and listen. No longer label makers, going beyond left or right, conservative or liberal, Democrat or Republican, and working together for the future of our great nation.

Snyder ends his treatise with a quote from Hamlet. "The time is out of joint. O cursed spirit, /That ever I was born to set it right.....Nay, come, let's go together."

45's Version of Imagine

Imagine there are no Muslims
It's easy if you're white
No blacks, or immigrants
Around us only light

Imagine all the people living to hear what I say.
Imagine there is only one country
It isn't hard to see
No welfare or anyone poor
Only the rich, those just like me

Imagine all the people living to serve me
You may say I'm a dictator and
No, I am not out of line
I hope some day you'll bow to me
And the world can be all mine

Imagine I own all possessions
I wonder if you can
No need for truth or kindness
A brotherhood called the Klan

Imagine all the people giving me all they own
You may think I am joking
It's only a matter of time
I hope someday you'll succumb to me
And the world will be all mine

Trying To Make Sense Out of Nonsense

Regardless of one's political bent, the proliferation of fake news is perplexing. It is hard enough to find an unbiased news source without having to vet news to determine if it is valid. How many times have you seen a post on Facebook or Twitter that goes viral, only to find it is not accurate? A great example of this was the news story about voter fraud in Ohio which was a fake news story created by Cameron Harris[23].

At the same time, to be accurately informed a person needs to get news from more than one source. This is probably the best defense against fake news or biased reporting. If you only watch Fox news or only read the New York Times, the information you have will be leaning right or left, while the truth lies somewhere in between.

The media has not helped this problem. Often, a news headline will be nothing like the story that follows, or the story will not be as sensational as the headline promised. An example of this was a recent

---

[23] The New York Times, January 18, 2017, article entitled "From Headline to Photograph, A Fake News Masterpiece."

story that had the headline[24] - "Reverse mortgages cost some surviving spouses their homes". The article then describes a woman who lost her partner and is now in danger of losing the home they shared. They were not married and the house was only in her partners name. Our news sources have stepped away from the who, what, when, and why of solid journalism[25] and have traded in-depth reporting for sound bites. Social media has not helped, as it has been training all of us to think in 140 character sentences or quick, short posts.

All of this has led to opinions that are uninformed or biased, or just not valid. Yet, we all have them and seem to not hesitate to express them. Again, social media has not helped, giving us not only a platform to express ourselves, but allowing us to express opinions virtually anonymously. This last factor has the negative impact of people posting some pretty vile comments. Pick a topic, post an opinion, and watch the responses. Those that agree with you will say so, and those that don't will too. The scary thing to me is those that

---

[24] The Mercury News article. January 15, 2017, by Karina Iofee.

[25] Journalistics' article August 5, 2010 by Jeremy Porter entitled "Five Ws and One H: The Secret to Complete News Stories."

disagree can get mean and hateful to a degree that almost feels life-threatening.

The election of 2016 has brought all of this out in dramatic fashion. Trump supporters can't wait to get Obama out. Clinton supporters can't believe Trump will be our next president. Many people voted for the lessor of two evils, and many chose not to vote at all. There were Democrats and Republicans who voted for their party's candidate reluctantly. Both sides asking, "Is this the best we can do?"

Now that Trump has actually become president things have gone from bad to worse. As if fake news was not bad enough, now we have alternate facts. Trump's spoke-person, Conway, used this phrase in defending the new press secretary Spicer, who lied about the turnout on inauguration day. Pictures don't lie, unless photo-shopped of course, but the ones on CNN[26] were real. The theme of this presidency seems to be, if we don't like the truth, we will make up alternate facts (insert lies) that keep us looking good.

David Brooks wrote a New York Times commentary and called Trump a bumbling Captain

---

[26] Reuters article January 23. 2017 by Daniel Trotta entitled "Crowd controversy: The making of an Inauguration Day photo.

Chaos[27]. He said, "We've never had a major national leader as professionally unprepared, morally compromised and temperamentally unfit as the man who took the oath on Friday", (meaning 1/20/17). He ends by saying that "with Trump it's not ideology, it's the disorder."

So with fake news, alternate facts, and an incoherent, ranting president, how do we make sense out of nonsense? Now is the time for all of us to stay as informed as possible. Read! Question everything. Check several sources. Do as a newspaper would do and get at least two verifiable sources before believing information. Read and listen to opinions that differ from your own, try and understand where someone who disagrees with you might be coming from. Don't retweet or repost anything without checking it out.

Challenge falsehoods, counter with facts. Hold our elected officials accountable. I find it interesting that with 100 senators and 435 representatives, we only hear from a few on any given issue. There is an old saying, "the squeaky wheel gets the grease". We need to be squeaky wheels.

---

[27] The New York Times, January 20, 2017, by David Brooks entitled "The Internal Invasion."

If we fail to keep the nonsense separated from sense we will fall into the trap that George Orwell spoke of in the novel *1984*. (Interesting that January 21st was the anniversary of his death).

"The Party told you to reject the evidence of your eyes and ears. It was their final, most essential command....And if all others accepted the lie which the Party imposed – if all records told the same tale – then the lie passed into history and became truth."

Abnormal Can Never Be Normal

The dictionary defines abnormal as, "deviating from what is normal or usual, typically in a way that is undesirable or worrying". If there is anything that can be said about the 2016 election and post election, it is that it has been abnormal.

Beginning with Trump becoming the Republican nominee, to the surprise of just about everyone, to him becoming the president-elect, as an even bigger surprise, nothing about any part of the election has been normal.

Debates, normally designed to reveal a candidate's position on issues, became displays of inane rhetoric. Media coverage, normally digging into a candidate's qualifications, became simple reports of outlandish statements and tweet analysis. A voter's choice, normally between qualified candidates, became the choice between two evils: the devil you know, or the one you don't.

In the introduction to the Federalist Papers, published in 1788, Alexander Hamilton wrote:

"It has been frequently remarked that it seems to have been reserved to the people of this country, by

their conduct and example, to decide the important question, whether societies of men are really capable or not of establishing good government from reflection and choice, or whether they are forever destined to depend for their political constitutions on accident and force. If there be any truth in the remark, the crisis at which we are arrived may with propriety be regarded as the era in which that decision is to be made; and a wrong election of the part we shall act may, in this view, deserve to be considered as the general misfortune of mankind."

While Hamilton was talking about whether or not the States should ratify the new Constitution, the quote can be applied to our current situation. Now that the results are in, the question for us is whether or not we are going to allow things abnormal to become normal. One of the most troubling issues is the seemingly "normalization" of Trump.

Degrading women is abnormal. To set aside remarks as "locker talk", to say "get over it", is not normal. An example is being set that is to the detriment of not only women, but society as a whole.

Mocking the handicapped is abnormal. Not only that, it shows an ignorance and lack of humanity of anyone who engages in it. To let it slide is inexcusable.

Categorizing anyone, based on race or religion, as criminal or un-American is abnormal. The fundamental rights of just being human, have been attacked and denigrated.

Ignoring the truth, by making false statements, is abnormal. The rise of fake news is bad enough, but when supporters don't care if a candidate blatantly lies it's deplorable.

To believe himself to be smarter than our intelligence services and not needing their expertise is abnormal. This is exactly how Bin Laden was able to attack us, by George W. Bush ignoring intelligent experts.

For a foreign government to interfere in any way in our electoral process is abnormal. Yet, there are those who either deny it or just say "let us move on, we are past that". Not only is it an act of war, but is solid grounds for dismissing any person involved (see Federalist Paper #68).

Anyone of these are unacceptable in a country that prides itself on freedom, liberty, and justice for all. But to see all of them becoming normal is not only extraordinarily worrisome but undesirable to the max.

A portion of the nation has elected a man who by all accounts, including the above, is abnormal. What is scary to me, is the attempt by so many to normalize him.

Opponents who once described Trump as unfit, a joke, are now groveling at his feet. A media that should be digging deep into so many reasons Trump *is* a joke, are hovering in a corner afraid to challenge him (although that may be changing[28]). Democrats and Republicans are playing a wait-and-see game, when they should be demanding accountability for his actions, even before he takes office. Leaders in the tech industry are meeting to "build a bridge" with him. Unfortunately that will be a one way road going in his direction only.

It is normal for a candidate to make promises he/she may not be able to keep. It is abnormal to completely back pedal on all one's promises by simply saying, "That was for show". He's making fools of the American people.

This is not about the election per se, nor the electoral process, nor being Democrat, Republican, or any political affiliation. It is about what we as a nation are going to consider normal. What we want our nation

[28] Newsweek, December 13. 2016 article by Kurt Eichenwald entitled "Donald Trump's Business Ties Are Already Jeopardizing U.S. Interests."

to stand for. It is about whether we will remain silent to the detriment of the very foundation on which this country was built and allow abnormal to become normal.

One last thought:

When I was in the military we had to follow the chain of command. We had to memorize the chain and obey orders from any superior. We were taught to salute any officer above us, not the man/woman but the insignia on their shoulder. This was and is the norm in the military, to respect the authority of the position. Thankfully, I am no longer in the military. The Commander-In-Chief is at the top of that chain. The one about to take that position does not have my respect nor am I going to normalize him and address him as president. Abnormal will never be normal.

High Treason

This election has been one of the most divisive in our nation's history. Yet, history tells us some have been worse as far as rhetoric and consequences (the election of 1828 has been labeled the worst[29]). On the surface, the battle between Trump and Clinton was one of Republican vs Democrat. Scratch just a bit and it is easy to see Clinton lost because she failed to address middle America. It is easy to forget as a Californian, how different a large part of the country feels about the government. When you have lost your job and your family, friends, and town are all struggling, and you blame the government, you are ready to vote for something different. States who in the past voted Democrat, voted Republican.

All of this would be fine if the winning candidate had been just about anybody but Trump. Because of his campaign rhetoric, he exposed the dormant hatred, racism, and bigotry that has always existed, but is now legitimized. The race for the oval office became a vote

---

[29] For a light-hearted discussion about this election, check out the Youtube video by Laughing Historically, October 23, 2012, entitled "The Worst Election in History: Andrew Jackson vs. John Quincy Adams."

for the soul of America. Who are we as a nation?, became the question that needed to be answered. The answer goes against what this nation has always been, not only to its citizens but to the rest of the world.

The mantra today is "the election is over, let us unite and move on". Leonard Pitts Jr. in his column on 11/15/16 responded to this call better than I ever could. As he says, if this were just about politics, then maybe we could unite and move on, but it is not. To quote the last part of his column[30], *"It's time the majority that believes in a progressive, inclusive and compassionate America did more than just tweet about it. Nothing wrong with tweeting, but forces of exclusion, hatred and rage have overtaken the highest office in the land, so it's also time for some old school activism. Time to march. Time to assail lawmakers. Time to boycott. Time to stand and be counted. Enough is enough. Let's take our country back."*

While I agree with what Leonard said, to me many who voted, or failed to vote, undermined the country. In my mind they committed high treason.

If you are black and voted for him not her, you are a traitor.

---

[30] Miami Herald, November 16, 2016, "I'm not in the mood for 'unity'. At the end of the day, Trumps's still a bigot."

If you are Latino and voted for him not her, you are a traitor.

If you are female and voted for him not her, you are a traitor.

If you did not vote for him or for her, you are a traitor.

If you did not vote at all, you are a coward.

If you are a Christian and voted for him not her, you are a hypocrite.

Black is a traitor to all who have gone before, who suffered to fight for civil rights, for justice, to Rosa Parks who stood her ground. You have sent yourself to the back of the bus.

Latino is a traitor to all their countrymen, so easily labeled rapists, murderers, criminals. To those who wish a wall will never be built you have told them, "I have mine, too bad for you, amigo."

Female is a traitor to all who have gone before, the women that fought for your right to cast your ballot, the women who fought for your right to choose. The women who refused to be less, refuse to give up their dignity. You have sent yourself back to the kitchen.

The voter of neither him nor her is a traitor, your ballot was wasted, you really voted for him, your moral stance was for naught, morality lost. Your message is silenced.

The non-voter is a coward, how dare you sit on your ass, the nation deserves more, the founding fathers are appalled, you gave up your right to be called an American.

Christians are hypocrites, for you have denied Christ. He loves, you hate. You have crucified Him again. You quote His Word, His Word quotes back, "Jesus wept."

Treason is defined as betraying one's country, but it is also betraying someone or something. Sadly, if you are in one of the above categories, you have also betrayed yourself.

America: On The High Road or Making A U-Turn

"....when they go low, we go high..." —Michelle Obama

My first encounter with politics was in 1960. Kennedy was running against Nixon and I was in eighth grade. We were assigned a candidate, had to watch the debates and write a report. Mine was Nixon. The thing I remember most was the controversy of Kennedy being Catholic. The big question was, would he abide by the constitution or take directions from the Pope?

Then in 1964, my senior year of high school, Goldwater ran against Johnson. I spent many a night in our local Sambo's (yes, it was a real place - kind of a Denny's) arguing politics with a few friends. Most of the country was afraid of what Goldwater was saying, ironically much of what he spouted came true. Especially about Vietnam.

In 1968, when Nixon beat Humphrey, I was in the army on a Nike missile base outside of Philadelphia. What a year that was - Martin Luther King had been shot in April, Robert Kennedy in June, and George Wallace was a strong third party candidate. Vietnam was hot, the civil rights movement was struggling, and the Democratic convention was marred by riots. It was interesting that Nixon ran as the "law and order" candidate.

Over the years I have seen and heard presidential candidates from all sides as they try to win over the people of this country. What a president can do, or not, depends a great deal on his/her relationship to Congress. It seems that over the last twenty years there has been more division than cooperation.

This election is the most divisive of my life time. Not so much Republican versus Democrat, but who we are as a nation. This election can define what it means to be an American, what America stands for, and what lies ahead for this country. I do not recall any other election that had the potential of destroying the foundation on which this nation was built.

We have been, and hopefully will continue to be, a diverse nation. Yes, there have been times when groups were segregated, minorities maligned, those different persecuted. But, while some of that exists, and probably will as long as humans do, overall we have moved past those divisions and coexist as Americans.

We, as I love to do, can argue viewpoints, disagreeing on issues, but then turn and work side by side to accomplish that which needs to be done. This is one of the things that has kept America strong.

Our rights, regardless of gender, religion, sexual orientation, race, or politics are protected in word and the more diverse we become, the more we all need to see that protection is ensured in reality and does not erode.

This country has a lot of issues. Issues that need to be intelligently discussed and solved. But like the song says, "if everybody is talking and no one is listening", solutions are impossible.

For me this election comes down to a choice. Continue to work on issues together, respect each of our differences, protect individual rights, and take the high road. Or, make a u-turn and give in to bigotry, hate, fear, divisiveness, essentially erasing all that has made this country great.

And here is the crux of it all. No matter what you think, our next president will either be Hillary Clinton or Donald Trump[31]. I know there are other people running that seem more appealing to some and I agree the top choices may not be the best. I understand not voting for either, or even not voting is sending a

---

[31] This blog was written on October 30, 2016 prior to the election.

message. The truth, however, is that this race is closer than anyone could have predicted. If this nation is to take the high road then Trump needs to be defeated. A vote for anyone other than Clinton, makes that too much of a possibility to even think about.

When all is said and done, I hope we will be on the high road. U-turns never get us ahead.

Fear & Ignorance 2, Love & Intelligence 0

'Fear is the only true enemy, born of ignorance and the parent of anger and hate." Edward Albert

Two major events occurred over the same few weeks that have one thing in common - both were fueled by fear and ignorance. Misinformation overcame facts, fear overcame concern for one's fellow human being. The first event was Donald Trump's rise to being the Republican nominee for President of the United States. (Just typing that sentence caused the hair on my neck to stand). The second event was Britain voting to separate from the EU by 52 to 48 per cent .

The fear of immigrants, especially Muslims, was a primary factor in both of these decisions. Mr. "Build a Wall", based a large part of his campaign on promoting the idea that America is under siege and we need to essentially close our borders. The pro "Brexit" proponents used the fear of refugees to convince many to vote for separation. This statement as to why some Brits voted to leave the EU could as easily apply to why some supported Trump's rhetoric about our immigrants - "They played up fears of ISIS attacks, of overburdened schools and hospitals, of moms, dads, brothers, sisters, children, and grandchildren forced to miss out on their rightful and paid-for state support, edged out by newly arrived migrants hungry for handouts and everything for free."(CNN) [32] The truth of how both countries benefit from immigrants was lost. It is almost laughable in the U.S. to hear immigrants denigrated when all of us, unless you are Native American, are immigrants.

Trump touts the slogan, "Make America Great Again", while the pro Brexit side shouted "Bring back the Britain of our memories". Both of these sound good, but what do they even mean? Trump's verbiage makes it sound as if we are not great. Au contraire, Sir Donald. Currently we have the lowest uninsured rate for health care ever recorded, an unemployment rate below five percent, and the longest streak of private-sector job growth on record, all while cutting the deficit by two-thirds. We have the best military in the world, the strongest economy, and one of the most diverse populations. Oh, maybe that last one is the reason for the cry from Trumpites and Brexitites.

---

[32] CNN.com, June 24, 2016, article by Nic Robertson entitled "A look at Brexit: Why are the Brits thumbing their noses at Europe?"

Blaming others for your problems is easy. Tossing out labels to dehumanize people is easy. Spouting bumper sticker slogans is easy. Creating fear with ignorance is easy. Taking the time to find the truth, caring for your neighbor, respecting one another, listening to all sides, being willing to stand together as human beings -- all take love and intelligence.

So far, fear and ignorance leads love and intelligence 2 - 0, let's just hope the game isn't over.

The Ignorance of Buzzwords

Words are amazing things. They can make us cry or laugh, make us happy or sad, make friends or enemies. George Carlin did a standup routine on the word *stuff*[33] which is hilarious. One of Robin Williams' best comic routines was the one about *golf*,[34] a true four letter word. One of the worst movies ever made was called simply *Gravity*.

Single words can create action. Tell a well trained dog to sit, or stay, or shake and you will see it sit on its haunches, or frozen in place, or extending a front paw. Yell "Quiet" in a crowded room and watch everyone go still, or "Fire" and watch them panic.

The problem with some words is that we assign meanings to them that are not based on facts. Our reaction to some words are based on bias or misunderstanding. What we think they mean, which often is a meaning without thought behind it.

Homeless is a good example. Say that word to ten people and you will likely get five different interpretations. Sadly, the majority will say it means

---

[33] See the Youtube video "George Carlin-Stuff."
[34] See the Youtube video "Robin Williams-Golf"-full version.

drug addicts or alcoholics or mentally ill. Here is a different thought, anyone who does not have at least six months income in the bank is potentially homeless. While there are those that are drug addicts, alcoholics, or mentally ill, the buzz word homeless does not define all.

When it comes to helping the homeless, however defined, and there is talk of a shelter in a neighborhood, the words that bring fear and trembling are "property values." The NIMBYs pull that one out every time to provoke a reaction of support to stop any thought of a shelter near them. Having been involved in setting up a homeless shelter in a residential area, I know this is a bogus argument, but fear can cloud the truth.

The gun debate is another heated issue that gets confused by buzz words. Mention gun control and the cry of "protect the second amendment, we have the right to bear arms", goes up. Funny that the words "well regulated milita" get lost in that debate. Any talk of gun control becomes, "they want to take our guns away". No one wants to listen to the words, "no they don't".

For a land settled and built by immigrants, it is almost comical that immigrant has become a negative buzz word. Add Syrian to that description and suddenly the word means terrorist. These words have the ability to create hate and fear so quickly, rational thought or discussion is almost impossible. Unfortunately, words are being used to build a wall causing division when we should be addressing our common humanity. Muslim becomes synonymous with ISIS, which is about as ignorant as saying all Christians are like the group from Westboro Baptist Church[35].

The terms liberal and conservative have become so mired in misunderstanding they are tossed about without any thought. The labels are so easy to use, thus ending any further conversation. He is liberal, so you can ignore what is being said. She is conservative, so she must hate everybody. These two terms are misused, abused, and overused. I love the irony that Jesus was the liberal who wanted to feed the poor and condemned the conservative Pharisees.

Buzzwords have become labels. If we can put a label on something or someone then we can put it in a box, put it on a shelf, and then there is no need to dig deeper. Therein lies the problem. In a society so used to quick answers, we have forgotten how to look for the truth.

---

[35] This so called Christian group puts out a newsletter entitled "God hates fags."

As long as we rely on buzzwords - prejudice, hatred, and ignorance will continue to divide us.

Dear Kamala Harris

The following is an open letter I posted to Senator Kamala Harris after hearing her talk about her candidacy for President. It fits all the current candidates on the Democratic side and could have been sent to any or all of them

Dear Kamala Harris:

First, let me say you would make a great president. Your intellect, demeanor, and political savvy would not only be a refreshing change to the current occupant but would serve you and this country well in your two terms. In a field that is getting crowded, you are my number one pick for the office of President of the United States.

Second, if I can be so bold, is a small bit of advice, if you are planning to rise above the crowd and take your seat in the Oval Office. Having heard you speak, both in interviews and in Senate hearings, there is one thing you need to change if you are to convince the nation you are the best candidate.

When you speak or answer questions there is no doubt as to your grasp of the facts or your stand on issues. The problem, one which Hillary Clinton had, is that you sound like a politician reciting talking points. I do not doubt you believe what you are saying, but there isn't passion behind your responses, they do not sound as if they are coming from your heart.

Alexandra Ocasio Cortez is an example of what I am talking about. She comes across as genuine, passionate, and heartfelt. Watch an interview with her and see what I mean. Another example is Chris Christie. While I may not agree with most of what he says, he too sounds like he is speaking from his heart.

Third and last, is that having heard your interviews, you, sometimes, fall into the trap of not answering the question. In a recent town hall, you were asked about solutions to DACA protection, and your answer talked about the broken promise to the young people and their parents by the current administration, but not your solution. On the positive side, in that same town hall when asked about student loans you had specific answers to solve the problem. This for me is a big issue in that when any politician launches into a diatribe in response to a question, it makes me feel they are not listening and are just trying to push their agenda.

In her book, "*Becoming*", Michelle Obama said she did not realize how stiff she was being until she saw clips of her speeches. She then went on to being herself and speaking more from heart. For you to pull in the nation to rally behind you, my hope is that you will do the same.

I am looking forward to 2020 when I can enter the voting booth, place an X next to your name and see you take over the office of the President of the United States.

Sincerely,

Don Grant

Progress

We thought we had progressed.
Turns out we have not.

Lessons of a jungle war
We thought we had learned,
Forgotten in poppy fields
Young lives, once again, spurned.
Marchers had marched
To set all men free.
Now black lives still don't matter,
True freedom yet to be.

We thought we had progressed.
Turns out we have not.

Women united, asking only
To be treated fairly.
Now, somewhat equal,
But only barely.
 Men had the power,
We thought we could do better.
NOW held the promise of change,

But men would not let her.

We thought we had progressed.
Turns out we have not.

Founded on liberty
All men are equal.
Sadly, our forefathers
Would not like the sequel.
United we stand
Divided we fall,
Once made us stronger
Now a reality call.

We thought we had progressed.
Turns out we have not.

Suffragettes got the vote,
Women rejoiced.
Men want to control their bodies,
Leave them no choice.
Good ole-boys
Ruled the day.
Ask any woman,
It's the same today.

We thought we had progressed.
Turns out we have not.

Inventions abound
Technology creates.
People are unhappy,
Filled with hate.
The American Dream
Once sought by all,
Now out of reach
As society falls.

We thought we had progressed.
Turns out we have not.

Our nation is a mess,
Our leaders have bowed out.
What we do next
Will be our greatest test.

If it is one, then it is all...

When I was in elementary school, one of my pet peeves was if someone in class acted up, the teacher would punish the whole class. Someone would throw a paper ball or a pencil and since no one wanted to confess, we all were made to miss recess or endure some other form of punishment. Because one person was "unruly", we were all considered "unruly".

In high school this mentality morphed into a dress code that said a male could not wear a tailed shirt untucked. If you did you were considered a "hood", because hoodlums dressed that way. My father had obtained a couple dozen white dress shirts for cheap and I wore one most days, untucked. Daily, I would have discussions with my teachers as to why they thought I needed to tuck in my shirt. My grades were good, I was not a hood, and to me the rule was pointless. I lost most of the time. It was either tuck in or go home. In the Army it was as bad. If one guy in the platoon did something wrong, we all suffered, usually by doing push-ups. This thought process of making the majority suffer for an act by the minority surfaces time after time.

Our world today is filled with examples. Someone jumps off the Golden Gate Bridge, solution - put up nets and ruin the view for all of us. One guy tries to light a shoe bomb, we all suffer the hassle of taking off our shoes when we go through airport security. Someone doesn't want to pay for car insurance, our rates are higher. Someone shoplifts, we pay more for products.

Sadly, this mentality is also the basis for prejudice, hatred, and misconceptions. Oh, you're a Muslim, then you must be a terrorist. You're a Christian, then you must be an extreme fundamentalist. You're a Democrat, then you must be a far left winger. You are a Republican, then you must be a far right winger.

We have become a nation of label makers. If we can slap a label on someone, then we think we know who and what they stand for. While this is an easy solution to dealing with each other, it is not only lazy but promotes ignorance, bigotry, and hate.

Yes there are Muslims who are terrorists, Christians who are extremely fundamental, far left Democrats and far right Republicans. For some reason we want to put one label on a group. I guess that just keeps it simple and comfortable for us, keeps us from having to think.

The homeless are a perfect example. The reasons for being homeless are as varied as the number of people on the streets. Yet, we would like to think they are all drunks, and addicts. If we believe that they are, then we can excuse ourselves from helping them, have a clear conscience when we just walk by them, ignoring their existence.

Not that this is the right attitude, as we should be doing more to help any person who finds themselves homeless. But, when you sit down and actually talk to someone on the street, look into their eyes, listen to what they have to say, you find an actual human being.

Apply this process to anyone. If you are a Christian, sit down with a Muslim and have an intelligent discussion. A Democrat, sit down with a Republican. On the far left, sit down with someone on the far right.

Somewhere along the line we lost the ability to hear each other out, and actually find out what someone else stands for, what they really think.

Maybe we have never had the desire.

Facebook has widened the divide, enhanced our ability to just label and carry on as usual. I constantly see posts putting down liberals, conservatives, Democrats, Republicans, Christians, Muslims, gun owners, anti-gun owners. The ability to say something derogatory about a group is made all the easier by not having to be face to face.

We all can't be right, we can't block out ideas that we may disagree with, we can't ignore a person or group that might think just a little differently than we do, we can't live in a constant state of fear of other people.

Behind every label we may use, there is another human being, not that different from ourselves. It is complete arrogance to think that we are better than someone else because of those labels.

As long as we stay comfortable with our narrow views, the issues and problems that face all of us will just keep getting worse.

Imagine if we had a national reconciliation day, where each of us had to sit down over a meal with someone we labeled as different from ourselves.

Would we all be better off?

Would hatred diminish?

Would the world be a better place?

What would happen if we all accepted one another, acknowledged and respected our differences, realized we are all in this together?